For Brianna, Will, Rachel, Justin, and Trevor—with love

—L. V.

For my father, William Francis Ryan. My first art teacher.

If only we could sit on his patio, one more time together, looking at the butterflies.

—E. R. E.

Sleeping Bear Press™

2395 South Huron Parkway, Suite 200, Ann Arbor, MI 48104
www.sleepingbearpress.com
© Sleeping Bear Press

Printed and bound in the United States.
10 9 8 7 6 5 4 3 2

Library of Congress Cataloging-in-Publication Data
Names: Vander Heyden, Linda, author. | Ewen, Eileen Ryan, illustrator.
Title: Mr. McGinty's monarchs / Linda Vander Heyden ; Eileen Ryan Ewen.
Other titles: Mister McGinty's monarchs
Description: Ann Arbor, MI : Sleeping Bear Press, [2016] |
Summary: Mr. McGinty and his dog Sophie love observing Monarch caterpillars and
butterflies on their morning walk, so when they discover that the milkweed
Monarchs need to survive has been mowed down, Mr. McGinty comes to the rescue.
Identifiers: LCCN 2015027645 | ISBN 9781585366125
Subjects: | CYAC: Monarch butterfly—Fiction. | Butterflies—Fiction. |Caterpillars—Fiction.
Classification: LCC PZ7.1.V395 Mr 2016 | DDC [E]—dc23
LC record available at http://lccn.loc.gov/2015027645

Mr. McGinty's Monarchs

By Linda Vander Heyden AND Illustrated by Eileen Ryan Ewen

PUBLISHED BY SLEEPING BEAR PRESS

On lazy afternoons, Mr. McGinty watched monarchs dip and rise on the summer breeze. With his magnifying glass, he studied them sipping sweet nectar from the flowers.

And when Mr. McGinty and Sophie went for long walks, he marveled as monarchs flitted and fluttered from milkweed to milkweed laying eggs.

"Milkweed's the only plant a monarch uses to lay its eggs," he told Sophie.
"When the eggs hatch, the caterpillars feed on the leaves. What d'ya think of that?"

Sophie's tail thump, thump, thumped.

Summer slipped by quickly. One morning, Mr. McGinty awoke with Sophie's warm breath on his face. "C'mon, girl. Let's check on the monarchs!"

When they reached the stretch of road where the milkweed grew thick, Mr. McGinty's shoulders drooped. His lower lip trembled.

All the beautiful plants lay on the ground.

Mr. McGinty examined the cut stems.
Monarch caterpillars clung to the drying milkweed.
Some stretched their striped bodies, searching
for a place to climb.

Hurrying home, Mr. McGinty loaded an old wagon with jars. Its rusted wheels squeaked as he pulled it from the shed.

"Hurry, Sophie!" he called. "We're going on a monarch mission!"

Squeak-creak ... squeak-creak ... squeak-creak ...

Mr. McGinty carefully picked up each monarch caterpillar.

"Betcha didn't know these little wigglers are also called larvae, huh, Soph?"

Sophie sniffed at a caterpillar.

Cars slowed. People shook their heads.

"Lot of fuss over some fancy worms," one woman said.

Mr. McGinty paid no heed. With gentle fingers, he lifted each leaf and lowered each larva. Soon his jars were full of wriggling, wiggling, stretching caterpillars.

"Time to go home, girl."

He patted Sophie's head.

Mr. McGinty, Sophie, and the wagon full of wriggling, wiggling, stretching caterpillars rolled along.

Squeak-creak … squeak-creak … squeak-creak …

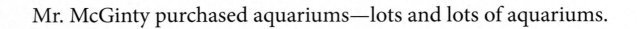

Mr. McGinty purchased aquariums—lots and lots of aquariums.

He lined the bottoms with sticks and milkweed leaves.
He placed the caterpillars inside and covered each
aquarium with a screen. Stroking Sophie's ears,
he watched the caterpillars feast on fresh leaves.

Mr. McGinty slumped into his chair. "How will we ever take care of all these caterpillars, Sophie? They'll need fresh milkweed leaves every day. They'll need someone to watch them as they grow. And someone to release them after they become butterflies."

Mr. McGinty sat up straight and snapped his fingers.

"Sophie!" he said. "I've got it!"

The next morning, he and Sophie loaded the truck with caterpillars.
They drove to a nearby school. Mr. McGinty taught the children
about the life cycle of monarchs—
from eggs …
to caterpillars …
to chrysalises …
to butterflies.

"When these caterpillars become butterflies," he said, "they'll migrate!"

He left an aquarium of wriggling, wiggling, stretching monarch caterpillars with each classroom, so the children could feed and care for them.

At the end of the day, Mr. McGinty had one aquarium left.
His eyes sparkled. "Looks like this one's coming home with us, Sophie."

Every day, Mr. McGinty fed the caterpillars fresh milkweed leaves.

The monarch caterpillars grew …
and grew …

They formed chrysalises … until finally …

When the monarchs had straightened their wings
and were strong enough to fly, Mr. McGinty
rolled out the old wagon one more time.

*Squeak-creak … squeak-creak …
squeak-creak …*

"Ready, Sophie?" Mr. McGinty laughed.

"Woof!" Sophie danced around his feet.

They joined the children on the playground. Together, they lifted the screens from the aquariums. One after another, monarchs spread their wings and flew ... up ... Up ... UP!

An early autumn breeze brushed against Mr. McGinty's cheek. He watched as monarchs fluttered, feather light, across the field.

"They have a long way to go," said Mr. McGinty. "But they'll be back."

Sophie licked him on the nose.

"And we'll be here to welcome them home."

Monarchs & Milkweed

Monarchs need milkweed to survive. Milkweed is the only plant a monarch caterpillar eats. It is the only plant a monarch butterfly uses to lay her eggs.

A monarch lays many eggs, but usually only one on each milkweed plant. A monarch egg is about the size of a pinhead.

When the tiny caterpillar emerges, it eats the egg sac. Next, it munches on milkweed. At first, it carefully chomps in small circles, so its mandibles (a fancy name for jaws) don't get stuck together with milkweed sap.

Milkweed sap is sticky and contains a chemical that is toxic. But it does not harm the caterpillar. Instead, the caterpillar becomes toxic too, and most predators leave it alone. This protection continues even after the caterpillar becomes a butterfly!

As the monarch caterpillar grows, it eats—A LOT! What goes in must come out, so it makes lots of poop, called frass. The caterpillar will outgrow and shed its skin five times before becoming a chrysalis!

At last the butterfly emerges from its chrysalis. It sips nectar from flowers through a hollow tube called a proboscis. Having a butterfly proboscis is like taking a straw with you wherever you go! A monarch butterfly drinks nectar from many flowers, including the flowers on milkweed plants.

Milkweed is disappearing. Many people don't understand how important milkweed is for the monarchs' survival. It is often cut down or sprayed with chemicals that kill weeds.

We can help monarchs by planting milkweed. This will give the butterflies a place to lay eggs. It will also provide food for the caterpillars. We can grow native flowers, so monarch butterflies have nectar. And we can ask grownups not to use sprays that kill weeds and insects.

A Monarch's Migration

In North America, monarch butterflies migrate every year. They cannot survive icy winters in the north. So in late summer and early fall, they fly south where winters are milder. Then they return north the next spring.

Not all monarch butterflies migrate. The generation of monarchs that we see earlier in the summer live only 2 to 6 weeks. They feed on nectar, mate, and lay eggs. It takes about 30 days for a monarch to grow from an egg to a butterfly.

Monarchs emerging from their chrysalises in late summer and early fall do not mate or lay eggs. They save their energy for the long migration ahead. Some will fly up to 3,000 miles (4,828 kilometers)! These monarchs can live up to 8 months. They are often called the super generation!

Monarchs living west of the Rocky Mountains spend winter in small groves of trees along the California coast. Monarchs living east of the Rocky Mountains fly south to the mountains of Mexico, where they roost in oyamel fir trees, protected from harsh weather.

In spring, these same butterflies leave Mexico and fly to Texas, mating and laying eggs along the journey. Their offspring will continue north, feeding along the way and laying more eggs. It can take several generations to reach the northern United States and Canada. It is the super generation's great-great-grandchildren that will begin the next journey south!

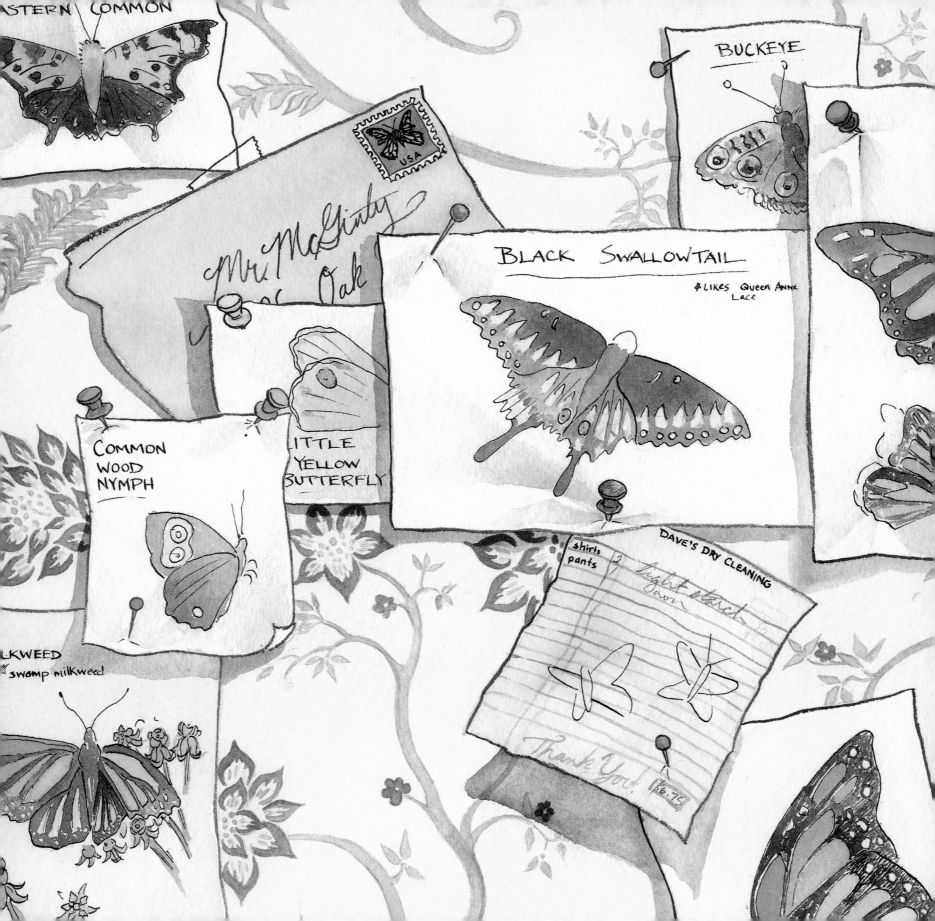